GOD'S WILL

GOD'S WILL

V BALAKRISHNAN

ZERO DEGREE PUBLISHING

Title: God's Will
Author's name: V Balakrishnan
Copyright © V Balakrishnan 2023
Published By: Zero Degree Publishing

Zero Degree Publishing
No. 55(7), R Block, 6th Avenue,
Anna Nagar West,
Chennai - 600040
Ph: 89250 61999

e mail: zerodegreepublishing@gmail.com
website: www. zerodegreepublishing.com
Printed in India.

First Edition by Zero Degree Publishing:
ISBN: 978-93-95233-11-8
ZDP Title: 58

Cover Design: Karthik Gowrisankar and Meera Sitaraman
Cover Photo: V Balakrishnan
Typeset: Vidhya Velayudham
Printed at Manipal Technologies, India

For Vikas Kyatsandra,
Your love, friendship and patronage made much
possible.

The play has been inspired and informed by newspaper reports of a true event. It has undergone some changes since it went on stage, and in that aspect, it's a little different from the version that won the award, but for the better. This is the tenth play of mine that is being published and I am very happy that the milestone number belongs to God's Will, *one of my favourite plays.*

V Balakrishnan

Characters

Dheera - Victim's mother
Satya - Victim's father
Policewoman
Policeman
Old Woman - Neighbour of Dheera and Satya
Madam - Minister's wife
Dhwani - Madam's political consultant
Someone*
Sanitation Worker*
Photographer*

*Characters can be played by the same person.

The play was first performed in July 2022 at the Alliance Française of Madras with the following cast and crew:

Dheera – Janani Narasimhan
Satya – Ganapathy Murugesan
Policewoman – Shakthi Ramani
Policeman – Karthik Gowrisankar
Old Woman – Preethi Bharadwaj
Madam – Shivangi Singh
Dhwani – Neeharika KS
Someone, Sanitation Worker, Photographer – Meera Sitaraman

Design and Direction – V Balakrishnan
Production Executive – Meera Sitaraman
Lighting Design – Aparna Kumar
Music – Srivaralaxmi Maya and Preethi Bharadwaj
Backstage Assistance – Megha Salila

The play opens on a group of people chanting and holding placards that read, *"Jab tak insaaf na hoga… beti ka sanskaar na hoga!"*[1]

Someone

I read this story in Valmiki's Ramayana but scholars say it's an interpolation, not part of the original. Once King Rama was challenged by a *brahmana*[2] whose five-year old son had died. Now in those days no one died before time, so the brahmana was convinced that the leader of the country was at fault, guilty of some great wrong because of which children were dying young. He and his wife threatened to give up their life by fasting and make the king face the heinous crime of *brahmahatya*[3] if he did not redeem the situation. The king consulted his council of eight wise men and they concluded that somewhere in the kingdom, a *shudra*[4] was

---

1 'Till we are denied justice, the funeral pyre won't be lit.'
2 Member of the first class of the traditional varna system.
3 Murder of a member of the first class of the traditional varna system.
4 Member of the fourth class of the traditional varna system.

practicing tapas—penance—and that travesty was causing these unfortunate things to happen. So the king climbed his aerial chariot and found the shudra near a pretty lake, who hung head down from a tree, desirous of becoming a celestial through austerities. The king cut his head off and amended the order of things, protected dharma, and the brahmana's child came to life.

Scene 1

(Dheera's home.)

Policewoman

(Sipping a glass of water.)

Ask the girl's father to cremate the body... How long do you think this *dharna*[5] and shit can last, huh? Once the media moves on... all will vanish... Make him cremate the body, it's his duty. You folks cremate, don't you? In such matters it's better... give it to *Agni*[6]... It is our dharma... Don't worry about the funeral costs... We will take care of everything. Dheera, you don't have the strength to tackle all this muck... Your husband and relatives have caused the city's traffic to come to a standstill... All traffic had to be diverted from the Minister's house... It's a government building... you know that, don't you? You think we can't arrest your men for creating a nuisance? Threatening the

---

5 Political Strike.
6 The God of Fire.

security of the Minister? ... But we don't want to cause you any distress... not with that young girl's dead body lying there... Tomorrow you will be shitting your pants when they slap a case on you for disturbing the peace and the police come knocking on your door. Listen to me carefully, quietly do the last rites... in the evening... best time... I will arrange for a mortuary van and the firewood... and a priest if you need one. I can get one from your own community... Give the girl's soul some peace. Dheera, they sent me to talk to you, a woman. It could have been a few men too. You understand... don't you?

DHEERA

They pushed her out of the moving bus and then they pushed me out too... I begged the driver to stop... he sneered and drove faster.

POLICEWOMAN

Speak what should be heard, Woman... Keep your mouth shut... It was an accident. Otherwise, why would they spare your son? He too was on the bus, right?

DHEERA

He was in utter shock when he saw what was happening to us... First my daughter... then me... they slowed the bus a few metres away and asked him to get down. No one stopped to help us. I carried my daughter's body to the closest police station. I was bruised, and bleeding...

(Silence.)

POLICEWOMAN

You refused to pay for three tickets… Why get into a luxury bus if you didn't have money? Government buses run too, don't they? You want the comforts but won't pay?

DHEERA

We were very tired… We wanted to return before it was too dark. This bus was there. The conductor leaned out and asked us where we wished to go… I was hesitating… They said come. We got in… They wanted three hundred for three tickets. I told them, "My children are underage, charge half rate." They said it's an AC bus… Minister Saab's own fleet… Then one of them stared at my daughter and said, "No way she is underage… see how big she is…" *(Breaks down.)*

POLICEWOMAN

You expect me to believe the people in the bus stayed silent while all this drama was playing out? What was the driver doing? And why did you not get down if you felt it was unsafe? You went along with the drama, did you not? So the bus conductor would allow you to ride without tickets.

DHEERA

What?

(Silence.)

POLICEWOMAN

Woman to woman, don't get involved in this. You don't
want it.

DHEERA

On the dead body of my daughter, I swear… the conductor,
his helper, and the driver's assistant cornered us… The bus
was moving fast. The conductor thrust his hand inside my
daughter's kurta and said, "This is a full-fledged woman",
and they laughed… I slapped him and pushed him away…
My daughter was crying, my son was in shock. They started
groping me and my daughter. I screamed and shouted…
Not one passenger looked away from the film they were
watching on the television screen… My daughter tried to
move towards the front exit. They called us obscene names…
I begged them to stop the bus. They pushed my daughter
out and then they pushed me… from the moving bus…

(Silence.)

POLICEWOMAN

What happened, happened. What your husband is doing
is ridiculous… sitting outside the Minister's house with
the dead body on the road… Suddenly you are all freedom
fighters… activists… Why? Go to Delhi… like the
farmers… better coverage and support… Your refusal to
cremate the body will incur you sin. It's causing a whole
lot of embarrassment… Go and convince your husband
to cremate the body. The Minister will give you all some

compensation… Otherwise, you will be left with that rotting corpse and nothing else.

DHEERA

Embarrassing who? Who are we embarrassing? We are the victims. I lost my daughter…

POLICEWOMAN

You know how much trouble the common folk are having to go about their daily routine because your people have blocked the road? My children were two hours late to school because of the jam… the city is in a mess. The rest of the country is watching us like a roadside show… The dead body has started smelling…

DHEERA

It's my daughter…

POLICEWOMAN

Go and talk to your husband. Otherwise, we will take the body for a post-mortem… that's the procedure in such cases. Do the last rites, Dheera, give some dignity to your daughter in her death… Even the Minister will support your claims… move for compensation for you…

DHEERA

Why do you want to cut my child's body? What for? I am speaking the truth. We were attacked, molested, abused and they killed my child. Now you want to butcher her too... I don't want anything... I want those men to hang... I want justice.

POLICEWOMAN

Justice is not the best option here. Cremate her and let things be amicable. That is why the body was released to you... If you insist on a *case-vase*, we will need to file a complaint, and then we will have to do a post-mortem.

DHEERA

I know what will happen once we agree.

POLICEWOMAN

Play it smart, Woman... I have to leave now... I have spelt it out for you... *(Silence.)*
I can't guarantee anything, but if you convince your husband to agree to the cremation, it's a win-win... You will get something... some compensation. Otherwise, we will forcibly move him and send the body for a post-mortem... worse, we cremate her somewhere... Even your daughter's ashes won't reach you... *(Looks around at the poor conditions of the house.)* You have food to eat in the house? Looks like the stove has not been lit in ages. I can get some rations delivered if you like... I am with the local police station. Ask for me if you need anything. Think of me as your friend. What's happened has happened... Now see what needs to be done.

(Silence.)

DHEERA

Help me… my son… they are threatening him…

POLICEWOMAN

Let me see what I can do… ask him to stay indoors for a few days.

DHEERA

Those bastards? You must know where they are…

POLICEWOMAN

How will I know? They are missing… hiding somewhere… We will find them. (*An old woman enters with food on a plate.*) Yes, make her eat. (*Policewoman exits.*)

DHEERA

My daughter is lying dead… her flesh rotting… she would have been 14 this year. What did I do to suffer this fate? Have I ever coveted someone else's man, house or food? My daughter… I want her… I want my daughter back. Motherfuckers… how could they have the heart to push her from a moving bus? Whoresons… would they grope their daughters and sisters too? They are offering us compensation for the accident… accident… their mother's cunt. I want my daughter. They called her a whore… called her such horrible things… Oh God! What will I do? They kicked me out of the bus… When I picked myself up and went to look for her, I was praying she should not have broken her leg or anything… I was dreading going to a hospital and having to spend money on medicines… Her eyes were open, her kurta torn from the fall… first thing I covered her chest with my dupatta. I was shaking her… telling her, "We are safe… those bastards are gone."… Her eyes were lost in the clouds… she was not there… she was… I won't cremate her unless those arse-fuckers are punished… I want to see their organs rot… 'Missing', she says… that State's whore… How can they be missing? My daughter… my daughter… her father won't stir… my relatives won't budge… they will leave that road over my dead body. The police are worried her body will start rotting and stinking? … Why will it rot? She is a goddess. She won't rot… she will stay intact till those men are caught. She is a *Devi*[7]. I am telling you, her eyes could not be shut. The doctor tried it… he said it's strange, but he could not. My daughter is a goddess now… I want her back. Where is she?

Old Woman

Have something to eat, restrain yourself… be calm… things will get better.

Dheera

I will immolate myself in front of the Minister's house if my daughter does not get justice. Food does not go down my

____

7 Goddess.

throat. My husband and son have not eaten in days… I can't eat… No, I don't want food… I want my daughter back. My daughter… She was talking non-stop that night about how hungry she was… I promised to make her parathas when we reached home. She smiled and challenged her brother that she would eat three parathas… *(Breaks down.)*

OLD WOMAN

Enough… calm down.

<h2 style="text-align:center">Scene 2</h2>

Dheera

Don't enter my house.

Satya

What happened, Woman?

Dheera

Why did you cremate my daughter without telling me? I had to learn from our neighbours that you have conducted the last rites...

Satya

They threatened to take the body for post-mortem... to find out what all happened to her...

Dheera

Fuck their mothers! I will tell you what happened to my daughter... She was killed... thrown out of a moving bus.

SATYA

I sat with her body on the road for justice... Enough, Dheera... My daughter's soul was screaming for peace... I could not torment her anymore... Her body lying on the road... rotting... I...

DHEERA

Now have you received justice? Have they hanged those animals? Has the Minister resigned? He is the monster running those buses... is he not? How could you agree to the cremation?

SATYA

So what would you have me do? See my daughter's body putrefying... phlegm and pus ooze out of it? I agreed... because...

DHEERA

What?

SATYA

They have arrested those bastards... they surrendered.

DHEERA

So convenient... you agree to the cremation and they surrender. What? Were they pissing behind a tree when you agreed to burn our daughter's body... heard you and surrendered? *(Silence.)* Why did you not send for me...? Why did you not allow me to see her face one last time?

Satya

They insisted… it's immediate.

Dheera

Because I would have not allowed it… they knew… and you knew it better.

Satya

I have to think of our son.

Dheera

What do you mean?

Satya

They will give us compensation. They will give me a job in the government and later when your son is 18, he will be given a job too. They have promised to install a statue of hers in the Government Girls' School. Dheera… life has to go on. We have to think ahead.

Dheera

The men will be punished?

Satya

They are in remand.

DHEERA

Will they go to jail? The case against the Minister? Will those buses run again?

SATYA

There is no case. I have agreed to withdraw the case. *(Silence.)* I have sought a written assurance from the authorities that no harm will be brought to our family. They will give us security cover too… Police will protect us… *(Silence.)* I told them we are feeling threatened… *(Silence.)* The Minister said he will give a written undertaking of responsibility if anything happens to us.

DHEERA

Police will protect… us? Have you been eating shit? The Minister is the only one we have to fear… it is his bus fleet… his men… it is his government. What a laugh! He promises us security…

SATYA

Dheera… We don't have to suffer any more. The Minister was saying he will lend us a second-hand car so we don't have to travel by bus again…

DHEERA

When did you learn to pimp, Satya? You could have whored your daughter while she was alive, but to whore her after her death is unforgivable…

SATYA

We can't bring her back… She is gone… Now her statue will be put up in the Girls' School… When you will be called to identify the men in the police station… don't do it… The men must go free… Only then will all the offers stand.

DHEERA

… You are a pimp. I will fight for my daughter's soul… for her offenders to be punished…

SATYA

I have mourned amply for my daughter… Nothing happened… Only her body rotted in front of me… I have done what I feel is correct… Now you do what must be done to keep the family safe.

DHEERA

You drank your mother's milk or her piss?

SATYA

I drank her piss… satisfied? Don't identify the men… say anything you want… but they must go free, then we get all they have offered us… If you so want, we will leave this place… go to your village… settle there.

DHEERA

My village? No… I will go there to immerse her ashes

when those men hang for what they did… Where are my daughter's ashes?

SATYA

The Minister has ordered it to be immersed in the *Ganga*[8]… they are taking it by police van…

DHEERA

Our daughter's ashes… refused?

SATYA

They feared it might lead to some more protests and marches… there have been enough. I have had enough… I am tired.

DHEERA

Not even her ashes… they refused to give me her clothes when we went to take her body… I have nothing left of my daughter.

SATYA

We will have her memories… She will guard us forever. I said yes to the Minister… Now, all you have to do is say you don't know, when they ask you to identify the culprits.

DHEERA

Will you be able to swallow the rotis bought from the money

---

8 The holy river.

they'll pay you? I can't… I will not give up without a fight… I will not fail to identify those bastards… They will die at God's hands… that much is sure. *(Dheera exits.)*

SATYA

Enough with the curses and killings and fights… enough…

Scene 3

(At a tea shop outside the police station. Policewoman is sitting, sipping a cup of tea with biscuits. Policeman enters.)

POLICEWOMAN

You look tired… bleary-eyed… want a *chai*[9]?

POLICEMAN

No, I had one at the railway station.

POLICEWOMAN

Security detail? Express?

POLICEMAN

Must have been 1 AM… You know that lower berth near the bathrooms?

---

9 Tea.

Policewoman

The ticket examiner's berth? Of course.

Policeman

I stretched myself there. The TT was on his jaunts to make some money… and I could smell a sweet odour wafting from the bathroom…

Policewoman

Shit? Piss?

Policeman

No, this was different… nor was it cigarette… I walked over people sleeping near the door... and I clearly smelt *ganja*[10]... I waited outside the toilet, and after ten minutes the door opened… came out a girl… *salwar kameez*[11], dupatta, neat and clean… I was not expecting a girl… and even if it was to be one… what would you think?… Torn denims… T-shirt types, with a backpack or something… But this one looked like neat and clean, and respectable… I did not know what to say. I was sure she had been smoking a joint in the toilet, but I did not know how to ask… This was not a *jhalli*[12]… The girl looked me in the eye and smiled at me. I was bewildered. I was fumbling for words and she brushed by me and went into the vestibule. I was sure she had smoked

---

10 Marijuana.
11 Female attire.
12 A word typically used in colloquial Hindi, which denotes a girl who is not 'orderly'.

up in the bathroom… but I was not up to challenging her at all. Almost as if she knew what I was going to ask her, she showed me her palm, holding a tiny bit of pink soap, wet and slippery, as if telling me she was taking a shit and not smoking a joint, and to prove it she has the soap.

POLICEWOMAN

Maybe she had constipation… The ganja would be a good laxative…

POLICEMAN

Then sell it in the pharmacy. I will buy a few kilos…

POLICEWOMAN

She got away by mesmerising you…

POLICEMAN

With the image of her using that soap after cleaning her arse…

POLICEWOMAN

Tsk tsk… Why you getting angry? Even women shit…

POLICEMAN

No fear about the police because I have a piece of wet, well-used pink soap to create images of what happened inside the toilet… Think about it… a runny stomach makes you formidable against the city's best. I am sure if it had been a man or a jhalli, I would have slapped them around a bit and confiscated their stash.

POLICEWOMAN

You don't smoke or smoke up?

POLICEMAN

It's worth money.

POLICEWOMAN

You should have had the day off… Why are you here?

POLICEMAN

Identification parade… so I came in mufti… Those four who surrendered… my height, a few of them.

POLICEWOMAN

The mother is coming… Her statement will be recorded today too.

POLICEMAN

What is she saying finally? Heard they are being offered 25 lakhs as compensation?

POLICEWOMAN

Really? They held out well then. I had visited the mother… She was so shattered.

POLICEMAN

That man, what's his name?

POLICEWOMAN

Satya.

POLICEMAN

Satya… he sees the world for what it is… he knows he can secure his family's future with the Minister's blessings… The woman sees nothing beyond her daughter's dead body.

POLICEWOMAN

She is justified in demanding blood.

POLICEMAN

She won't be able to stand against all this.

POLICEWOMAN

I have been told to take her statement… What she says today will go to court…

POLICEMAN

And what will happen? These arseholes will go to jail you think?

POLICEWOMAN

Why not? Not like they are the Minister's relatives…

POLICEMAN

Then why are we protecting the buses?

POLICEWOMAN

What do you mean?

POLICEMAN

We have been riding alongside, providing security.

POLICEWOMAN

Still… Why should they not be punished for what they did? I am saying let's break their balls in lock-up… let's see how many women they try to molest after that…

POLICEMAN

You believe in the molestation story?

POLICEWOMAN

You don't?

POLICEMAN

I have been thinking about it… A bus filled with passengers… there is a movie running… people are up and about… won't anyone else have seen anything? Tried to protest or stop them?

POLICEWOMAN

When was the last time you protested when you saw a woman being groped in a moving bus or on the street? We may be the police... but we behave like them, don't we? No one likes confrontation... better to resolve it by talk or pretend nothing happened.

POLICEMAN

It's not like that all the time... I have had my fair share of confrontations... Remember when I almost beat up that man during *Diwali*[13]? He was stripping his wife in public, saying the sari she was wearing was bought by their neighbour. That she had whored herself for it... But we can't take any action without complaints and reports. We will end up trying to be Amitabh Bachchan and the woman will scold us for meddling in her domestic affairs.

POLICEWOMAN

There are people who have come forward. The cleaner... one passenger... the brother of the girl.

POLICEMAN

Why is the Minister so perturbed? Like you said, not his relatives... and he will look good if he steps up to get these arseholes punished... will be for the better in the elections... image and all.

---

13 Festival of lights.

Policewoman

No, you are thinking too straight… won't work that way…
it will backfire… ample and more fodder for the opposition
and it's not about how clean you are… it's about how good
you are at showing you are clean… Keep your pants stain
free… stink does not matter… farts are not tangible.

Policeman

I have a few tangible shitheads to parade with… I will check
on them…

Scene 4

(Dheera's home. Dheera is sweeping the floor. Satya enters.)

SATYA

Bitch… What have you done? We are lost… my son will be killed… they will rape you and make me watch. You whore! Why did you identify those men? It will be a court case now… you know what story they will push in our faces… that you and your daughter were soliciting in the bus, and when they confronted you… you both tried to escape by jumping from a moving bus… they told me in so many words… I will be branded my daughter's pimp. Whore, did I not ask you to shut up? The Minister was ready to give us money, jobs, land… our son's life would have been secured… You have killed us all.

DHEERA

You won't be able to watch me getting raped? I watched our daughter being abused… I was abused… I see you now abusing the memory of my daughter. What do you care about, but that filthy job and money? … Yes, you are a pimp. Satya, I don't care for your threats or beatings… I am resolved to die, but I won't allow those bastards to go free.

SATYA

I will see how you speak, when I have beaten your life out…

DHEERA

Why don't you beat the life out of those men, the Minister… What are you scared of? Dying? Die, Motherfucker… die honourably… I will cherish your memory along with my daughter's… No, you want to live… with land… money… You love your life… you will eat their shit and drink their spittle if they throw money at you…

SATYA

Dheera, enough! I loved my child… I am not selling her out… you stupid woman. We will be able to prove nothing… those men will go free and then they will come for us… I don't want to spend the rest of my life scared and running. Think of our son… how will he be able to go on with life if his legs are broken or worse… he is killed? I sat on the road with my girl's dead body… asking for justice… Slowly all those who gathered left. Whom did I gather around me? Vendors… salesmen… food stalls… it became a circus… I am not a beast, Dheera. I have lamented my fate, my destiny, my child… enough! I have my son to think of… What will he do if I am killed? You are killed? I am sure, Dheera, none of us will be spared… My daughter has died, but in her death she has made our lives comfortable. I beg you, Woman, take back your statement… let's take the money on offer, the land, the government job… let's leave this place… We will mourn our daughter's death for life… but don't make me mourn for more than that… I can't take it anymore.

DHEERA

Go… run away or hide somewhere… coward… I will fight for my daughter.

(Old Woman enters. Satya exits.)

OLD WOMAN

Dheera… quiet… What is all this? Don't embarrass Satya… everyone can hear you.

DHEERA

Why should I be bothered? You heard what he is insisting we do… accept their alms and forget what happened to my daughter? Mother, how can I live with it?

OLD WOMAN

Dheera… sit with me. Woman… calm down! You need to calm down first… listen to me… hear me out. I lost my husband and eleven members of my family in the *riots of 1984*[14]... we were slaughtered like animals, cut like carrots... Suddenly the streets we used to walk and play in had turned into a battleground... Hordes of men, brandishing swords and sickles... We were attacked, murdered and burnt... Later, I learnt that this mob was coming after attacking the Gurudwara where my husband *(Does not complete the sentence.)*... Like trapped animals, we tried to fend for ourselves... I was hidden in the house of my neighbours... Muslims... they saved two of my sons, removed their turbans and cut their hair with a pair of kitchen scissors... made them wear their children's clothes... I saw from a tiny window in front of me, girls and women being dragged to the streets, raped, and burnt alive... Men defecated on them, urinated on them, before setting them on fire... I lost everything... Amidst the smouldering embers of the aftermath of the attack, I was left with nothing... Herded from one rescue camp to another... The Gurudwara helped me... I know the fear that made me stay up and watch over my children each night... I know the fear that ripped my heart if anyone was late to return home... If I heard loud noises, I panicked... I had seen and survived the worst bestiality of humans, where dignity was ravaged first... then the body... and finally the soul... We came back here, to my ancestral place, once I had some money saved up... My sons still have anxiety attacks... I don't know where my daughters and my sister-in-law went... killed, burnt, sold... nothing. Every year, I fend questions from a new

---

14 The 1984 anti-Sikh riots, also known as the 1984 Sikh Massacre, was a series of organised attacks on Sikhs in India following the assassination of Indira Gandhi by her Sikh bodyguards.

journalist… What happened that night…? Do I feel justice was denied to me? How has life been without my husband? New journalist… same questions. Dheera, there is no justice for you and me… We cannot challenge them, Dheera. Ask me today what I want… to see those men who slaughtered us hanging or my sons happy and safe? I will choose my sons' happiness any time… This avenging of your daughter's death is your anger and ego, Dheera. Your husband is right… first learn to live, to fight another day… I lived through rabid mobs ravishing and burning and looting and killing… Nothing happened to those who perpetrated the crime… We, the victims, are scarred for life… We will pass these scars to the next generation… that will be our legacy. What you are facing today, Dheera, is a fraction of what we have seen. Don't be enslaved by your emotions. Take what is being offered and let your son and his children make a better life for themselves. Once we were attacked by those who did not belong to our community… the so-called other people… but today, it's our own community baying for our blood… Don't fall into the trap of valour, Dheera. Secure your family's future when you can. When a mighty tree falls, the ground around it shakes… The tree you want to bring down will end up crushing your own family… let its shade protect you… even if it's poisonous… Even to live with the memories of your daughter, you will need peace of mind… You can't spend your life glancing over your shoulder. I don't want that for you, Dheera. Listen to your husband… he is not being a coward… he is protecting his family.

Scene 5

(Dheera's home. Satya enters from outside with a stool and places it in the centre. Dheera enters from inside the house. The Policeman, Policewoman and Dhwani enter.)

POLICEWOMAN

How are you, Dheera?

DHWANI

Good you agreed to meet Madam. The Minister wanted to come too, but he had to leave for Delhi.

DHEERA

I did not call anyone here.

(Silence.)

POLICEWOMAN

Satya… where will she sit? *(The Policewoman looks at Dhwani, who gestures to her to let things be as they are.)*

Take this food… it's packed with plates and spoons. Just unwrap and serve it as it is. There is extra food for you all. Use the bottled water and the cups I have got… wash your hands before handling the food.

DHEERA

I don't want her in my house.

SATYA

Shut up, Woman!

POLICEMAN

Any sickles, knives, any weapons lying around?

SATYA

Only my implements…

POLICEMAN

Put it all in this sack and leave it outside in the jeep. Collect it after Madam leaves.

DHEERA

I don't want her in my house.

POLICEWOMAN

Dheera, behave and listen to what she has to say… don't make things worse for yourself…

DHWANI

Listen… maybe some good will come out of this for both the parties.

DHEERA

Why? Was her daughter molested and killed too?

(Dhwani receives a text about Madam's arrival. She exits.)

POLICEMAN

Dheera, watch your mouth… she won't be here long… just be civil and courteous.

(Madam enters and removes her footwear near the threshold. Dhwani enters with her.)

MADAM

All ok?

POLICEWOMAN

Yes, Madam.

(Madam places the stool aside and sits on the floor.)

MADAM

When the party president sits on the floor, who am I…?

POLICEWOMAN

Should I organise some chai… biscuits?

MADAM

No no… That food business is on na, Dhwani?

DHWANI

Yes, Madam, that's all arranged.

MADAM

You got extra for them, I hope.

SATYA

We don't dare…

MADAM

Eat it later… Dheera can be spared the stove today… We women know.

DHEERA

I don't want anything.

MADAM

Dhwani, I don't expect any media to show up. If they do, keep them away…

DHWANI

It is not in the official diary… We did not use the red beacon either.

MADAM

Satya, I did not use my car to come here. I did not want anyone to know I am visiting you… My husband was not too keen either… *(Dheera and Satya look sharply at Dhwani.)* But I know a woman's pain.

DHWANI

(To the Policewoman.) You said there is an old woman… living close… Some neighbour? Get her… we need one picture of her with Madam…

(Policewoman exits.)

MADAM

When this whole tragedy occurred… I was greatly upset. Then I went to the temple and prayed and meditated… I came back and told my husband with resolve, whatever happened was God's will… Have we broken the rules in getting the permit for the buses…? We may have… but did that cause your child to die? No… The four men who have been accused of abusing her… did they misbehave with your daughter and wife…? I don't know… but they will be punished for it either way… Will that bring your child back? No… Dheera, you are a mother and I understand your pain… your anger… but there is a lot more at stake here for me… more than the transport business, it's my political career. First time I am standing for the election… reserved seat… I am planning to get elected from the city. None of this will augur well for us… all your anger will destroy me… and I did not do anything. We advised you to withdraw the case… you refused. Now, it's too late to withdraw the case, but we can amend the situation… We won't bail them out. Let it come up… but when you do appear in court, you can make a difference to the way things have to happen. All you need to do is to go back on all you have said to the media and the police… So let it come up in court… where you can resolve it to everyone's satisfaction. My lawyer will give you clear details and instructions… You will officially get a good compensation, and we will top it up… Enough for you to live peacefully away from all this… and you deserve peace after all this trauma. Satya, you will get a government job… and on your retirement, your son will be employed in the same position… government job, pension, gratuity, everything… Do farming in your spare time… hardly any pressure in government work.

DHEERA

My daughter?

MADAM

We are having a statue of hers made, which will be placed in the Government Girls' School, and also two scholarships will be announced in her name... Your daughter is a boat which has pulled you all to the shore. (*Policewoman enters with the Old Woman.*) Who is this?

POLICEWOMAN

The neighbour... Dhwani madam wanted her here... for the photographs.

MADAM

Hmm... okay... okay. Sit down, Mother.

SATYA

We are not able to travel anywhere without apprehension and fear... My wife is not able to think of boarding a bus.

MADAM

Yes, we talked about it. Minister Ji will get you a car... not a new one... second-hand... Use that for moving around... (*To Dhwani.*) Shall we eat?

(*Dhwani acknowledges and looks to Dheera to bring the food arranged from inside. Dheera restrains her contempt and exits to bring the food. She places it in front of Madam.*)

MADAM

Finger bowl?

POLICEMAN

(To Dheera.) Plastic bowl with water…

MADAM

(To the Policeman.) I won't eat *jalebi*[15]… take it.

(Policeman removes the sweet and offers it to the Old Woman who stares at him. He puts it inside the remaining food parcels and leaves. Madam starts eating hesitatingly.)

SATYA

My son is being threatened whenever he steps out of the house.

MADAM

That will stop… We will do one thing… we will have a policeman around for a few days… Dheera?

SATYA

We don't want anyone to be punished…

DHEERA

Those men who put their hands on me and my daughter… I won't agree to them being freed.

---

15 An Indian sweet.

MADAM

What happened has happened… We cannot change anything… I told you those men will be punished for what they did… but I don't want a case… It's not about you agreeing or not… it's about whether you agree with all the gifts we are offering you… and we all stay happy, or the case happens and you lose all that I am offering… Of course, that kind of publicity will kill my career too… Dheera, your loss is tied to my loss, it affects my husband, me, and all the party work. I want to avoid it. I will deliver those men to you, tied up and stripped naked, do what you like with them… break their bones… take your revenge… but we cannot have a public case.

DHEERA

Where were you in 1984?

OLD WOMAN

Dheera…

MADAM

What?

DHEERA

1984, the riots in the Capital, where were you? Did you lose anyone in the riots? Anyone from your family raped, burnt, killed…? Lost any property?

MADAM

It was a sad phase for us all, but why are you asking me this?

OLD WOMAN

Woman, shut up!

DHEERA

Nothing… was just trying to understand what kind of compensation can be paid for negating one's memories…

OLD WOMAN

Dheera, enough! Listen to Madam, she is helping you…

MADAM

Your woman is losing it, Satya… Think hard about what I have said…

(Silence.)

DHWANI

Shall we proceed to call the photographer inside? A few photos of you eating in their house?

MADAM

Maybe some with a framed photograph of the girl… You have one? *(Satya exits to bring a framed photograph from inside. Madam gets up and moves towards Dheera.)* All you have to say is that there is no acrimony against me and whatever you were saying till now was fed to you by the opposition. You are happy with the steps taken by the government and you are assured justice will be delivered by the present government.

DHEERA

Deliver justice then.

MADAM

25 lakhs, land, job, car… What else do you want?

DHEERA

Let those men go to jail.

MADAM

Sure, but then you get nothing… *(Satya enters with the framed photo.)* and don't complain if your son comes to any harm.

SATYA

(To Dheera.) Shut up, Woman… *(To the Policewoman.)* Please, you call that photographer in.

(Dheera takes the framed photograph from Satya and storms outside.)

OLD WOMAN

Dheera!

(The Policewoman enters with a photographer. Dhwani instructs Satya.)

DHWANI

Serve it to Madam. *(A photograph is taken of Madam eating and Satya serving her plate.)*

DHWANI

Madam, one photo of you feeding him?

(A photograph is taken of Madam feeding Satya a morsel of food. Madam throws the morsel on the plate, washes her hands on the finger bowl with bottled water. Gets up to leave.)

DHWANI

Madam… *(Dhwani reminds Madam of the Old Woman. A photograph is taken of Madam touching the Old Woman's feet. Madam exits.)*

DHWANI

(To the photographer.) Do proper colour correction… Last time it was very dark.

Scene 6

(Dheera's home. Satya enters from inside and sits. Silence. Dheera enters with a bag of rations. She moves into the house. She comes back with a bag and realises that her lunch box has been leaking oil from its sides. She wipes clean the contents of her bag as she moves towards the threshold of the house.)

DHEERA

I have made rotis for you… eat when you want.

SATYA

Where did you go?

DHEERA

I went to collect rations for the four of us.

SATYA

Three of us…

DHEERA

I told them... They wanted to see the paperwork... Death certificate and a few more. The shopkeeper advised that we collect rations for the four of us. I didn't know what to tell him.

(Silence.)

SATYA

Why have you packed your food?

DHEERA

I have to go out.

SATYA

Where?

DHEERA

(Silence.)

SATYA

Where? I asked you, where? Where are you going, Woman?

DHEERA

The hearing is happening... I have been summoned... might take the whole day.

SATYA

Sit down.

DHEERA

I won't. I have to go there.

SATYA

Not happy with having killed our daughter, now you want to kill our son?

DHEERA

I killed my daughter?

SATYA

Yes, Bitch, you did! You killed my child. Now you are going to kill my son. Why spare me? Kill me too.

DHEERA

You are dead to me, Satya. You died long ago for me. How dare you accuse me of our daughter's death?

SATYA

Why step out of the house after dark? Why step out of the house at all? Don't I earn us food? That day I told you not to go out in the evening… You dragged the children with you… my daughter was sacrificed. How many times have I told you not to fight with men? Keep yourself covered… keep our daughter covered.

DHEERA

You bastard… She was only 13 years old… I know why you are spewing all these accusations… You have got used to licking the Minister's shit… You died as a husband for me… Now you are dead as a man too. Shame on you!

SATYA

They will kill our son if you go for the hearing.

DHEERA

My brave son would prefer to die fighting and avenging his sister's death than cower like his father… he did drink my milk.

SATYA

Dheera, don't… I will kill myself…

DHEERA

I have been cuckolded by the Minster… you have become his whore.

SATYA

Sit down, Woman… I have had enough of this battle. I am tired… My daughter is dead… leave her alone, please. I beg you. I don't want money or land… I just want to see my son grow up. I want to wake up tomorrow without fear… Dheera, if you take one step out, I will burn myself right now…

DHEERA

You burned our daughter without telling me… do this also without telling me. I mean it.

(Satya goes inside and enters with a canister of kerosene and proceeds to empty it upon himself.)

DHEERA

You don't have the balls…

SATYA

Dheera… don't do this… don't go… they will crush us like ants. Don't kill our son… don't leave me alone and go. I beg you! Please stay back… Dheera, I would rather burn myself and die, than take this any longer… Please, I beg you… don't go…

DHEERA

You have forgotten her, have you not? She is nothing to you now… just a ration card to get your freebies…

(Dheera exits. Satya goes inside and sets himself on fire. He screams. Dheera hears the screams, sees the flames and screams in shock.)

Scene 7

(At the hospital. Dheera enters with a plastic bag. The Old Woman is sitting outside the burns ward. A sanitation worker is cleaning the ward, who exits through the course of the scene.)

OLD WOMAN

Why are you holding on to the burnt clothes? Throw them away. *(Dheera moves towards the ward.)* Don't go in, the police are with him. *(Dheera comes and sits down next to the Old Woman.)* I will tell your son to eat at my home till Satya is discharged… I will bring you food too…

DHEERA

Mother, you don't have to…

OLD WOMAN

What's a few extra rotis to make… you take care of him…

(Silence.)

Dheera

What do I do, Mother?

Old Woman

What Satya wants… God be blessed, you saved him… Look inside… private room, best care, food and medicines… nothing to be paid for… The Minister has taken care of him, Dheera… Learn to protect what you have. This is no battle for righteousness you have to win.

Dheera

I did not go to the hearing… How could I…? Over Satya's burning flesh… Yes, he survived… Even when men immolate themselves… it is the women who have to undergo *agnipariksha*[16].

Old Woman

We are poor people… even an association with the upper class happens for us only by chance… otherwise, they don't even know we exist. Now the Minister is asking for your help… make use of this opportunity… take the money and live the rest of your life in peace.

Dheera

I have no peace… and I will have no peace till my dying day.

---

16 Trial by fire.

OLD WOMAN

But your man and your son will have peace… comfort… safety. Dheera, what do we want in the end? To be peaceful till our death comes beckoning… to die with our children and grandchildren around us. Leave these fights for justice to the privileged… ours is to live in silence… and die without inconveniencing anyone. Your daughter is not coming back… soon the trauma will be a memory… then with luck, it will fade away… Leave it. Once Satya is discharged, leave this accursed place forever… go to your village…

DHEERA

You have not forgotten till date what happened to your family. Why are you asking me to leave the one fight that's making me wake up each morning?

OLD WOMAN

I have forgiven everyone. All I want is for my sons to settle in Canada and be happy. Humans are innately good people… bad things happen… but so does the good… give goodness a chance and give yourself a chance. It's godsent… to own a farm and feel the sun on your back.

DHEERA

My daughter used to hide behind the door and gently peep out… she was not shy, but she wanted to see the world before it spotted her… and then slowly she would bring herself out… Satya would buy extra milk for her… he never showered that kind of love on our son, she was special to him… and now, she is reduced to being just a means to fulfil his dreams… What did I give birth to her for? To be abused and killed? How can this world be so cruel?

OLD WOMAN

There are too many of us… to be counted and accounted for… too many… Too many of us to be taken care of… What balance of this world gets tipped if a lamb is slaughtered? It's only food… Only the killing of a tiger will catch the attention of everyone… from poets to politicians… We are worse… too many in number… living in squalor… there to be fed upon… left to rot… to die in oblivion. Now, you have a chance… a chance to escape all this…

DHEERA

If we are born once, why should we die twice? Let us die and take them all with us, at least we can die fighting…

OLD WOMAN

Whose decision is that to be? Your husband and your son have a right to choose what they want from their lives… You believe your life has nothing left after your daughter died, but your family wants to live… You choose death, they choose life… whose balance is heavier? Don't destroy them because you are offended with the way the world is… We will kill… maul… ravish… that's who we are… If someone is providing a way out… then take it, Dheera. You are not alone in this… think of your family…

DHEERA

I don't have a right to choose death for others… my daughter and I… she was killed… Did they have the right to choose death for us…? Does my husband have the right to choose a life worse than death for me…? Fine… but I can't live with Satya after all this… I will do what he wants and go away…

OLD WOMAN

Where?

DHEERA

Where my daughter is…

OLD WOMAN

Don't be ridiculous! Think about your son…

DHEERA

He will survive… his father will have a job, land, and money. Mother, come with me to the court… after that I won't be coming back.

(Sanitation Worker enters.)

SANITATION WORKER

They're calling you inside.

(Dheera exits.)

Scene 8

(A room. Dheera and the Old Woman are seated. The police are with them. Dhwani enters.)

DHWANI

(To the police.) You may wait outside. *(The police exit.)*

(To Dheera.) Did you eat anything?
(Dheera shakes her head – No.)

(Dhwani prepares two plates with sandwiches, pours two cups of coffee and places them in front of the women. Dheera refuses the food.)

DHWANI

I insist, please... Dheera, before we go to the court, I want to make sure you are prepared... I am going to ask you some questions in the same manner you will be asked later... Let's make sure you have the correct answers... They will try to bully you... be stoic... stick to the answers we prepared. *(Opens her notes.)* Are these the men whom you encountered on the bus?

DHEERA

I was not fully conscious when the police took my statement... I was not very sure whom I pointed to...

DHWANI

You realise the accused will be set free if you change your statement...

DHEERA

I asked my son... he too was unable to identify the accused... It was night... It was dark inside the bus.

DHWANI

(Refers to her notes.) Dheera, those men were booked for murder under the Indian Penal Code and under the provisions of the Protection of Children from Sexual Offences Act... as well as Scheduled Castes and Scheduled Tribes Act... based on your statement. If you turn hostile, all of them will go scot-free...
Don't answer immediately... look confused... then respond with full eye contact.

DHEERA

We were pushed from the bus... but I can't with certainty say by who... We were not molested or anything.

Dhwani

Are you under any duress? Tell me this… on what basis had you earlier claimed that obscenities and lewd gestures were hurled at you before you were pushed out of the bus?

Dheera

I was unwell and don't remember.

Dhwani

Have you received a hefty amount? Is that why you don't remember anything anymore? …
Don't look scared, Dheera…

Dheera

I am mentally unwell… I don't remember anything…

Dhwani

What do you remember about that day? …
Take your time…

Dheera

I remember boarding the bus and having an argument over the ticket price. I fainted and the entire episode happened when I was not conscious. I don't know how my daughter and I landed on the road.

Dhwani

Will your husband know something about what happened?

Dheera

He is not aware... he was not even there... The student leaders made him tell some story they created.

Dhwani

You were summoned a few times for the hearing... Each time you refused to turn up, why? ...
This is an important question, Dheera. Here, you can break down... it will help... talk about your daughter... Sorry, I know it's harsh...

Dheera

I don't know why I did not appear... Whenever I think about April 29, I just remember me and my children boarding the bus. I handed over 100 rupees to the conductor for three tickets and we had an argument over the ticket price... I have no idea what happened after that. It's blank at the moment. I cannot recall if we were pushed off the bus or fell on our own.

Dhwani

Are you sure of the date? ...
Look confused...

Dheera

I think so... or maybe it was 27th... I am not sure.

Dhwani

Not sure which date your daughter died? ...

Break down again here… it's a good place.

DHEERA

Please, I am unwell… I don't remember. I am taking medicines… I don't know.

DHWANI

Are you sure you cannot identify the four men who are in custody?

DHEERA

I have never met them… we slipped and fell… on our own… I am sure.

DHWANI

I think we are good. Well done, Dheera. Do not forget what we practised… If there is any question we have not discussed… just say your medicines have numbed you, and you cannot be sure. Your husband, how is he?

DHEERA

He is okay…

DHWANI

What happened?
I know what happened… but what is the official answer you will give in court? You must tell the right thing.

DHEERA

I was cooking food… he sat too close to the stove… his *dhoti*[17] caught fire. We doused it immediately.

OLD WOMAN

He was very lucky… got away with some scars and scalding… This woman… she saved him… got burnt herself.

DHWANI

Good… good… *(Receives a phone call.)* Excuse me.
Yes, Sir… Yes, Madam had informed me you will be calling… I have had a talk with the mother and her story has been clarified… There won't be any problem… Acquittal should be done on the basis of lack of evidence. The mother has turned hostile. The bus driver… conductor and the two helpers will be set free honourably… No, no… the prosecution will have no evidence against our clients… No, Sir, none of them remember any details… See, two of the passengers who had recorded statements earlier, both have amended them to say they had front row seats and do not know what happened in the back. No… no… no… Sir… the father's statement makes no sense… the father was anyway not on the bus… I know he is recanting but let's avoid putting him on the stand… he is injured anyway… All statements will be recorded in the court of the Additional District and Sessions Judge… The son has been told to get there… Yes… The basis of the FIR was the identification

---

17 Indian drape for men.

of the four accused but all witnesses are hostile now, Sir…
I am taking her to the court now… prepped her, Sir… All
good… no issues, Sir. I will come down in the evening…
Madam has organised an all-night *kirtan*[18]. Yes, Sir, I will
keep you posted… And Sir, Congratulations.
(To the police.) Come in… *(Police enter.)*
Dheera, come… we must be on time. *(To the police.)* You
both may return to the station… I will be there with her…
Have some snacks… coffee is there too… hope it's not gone
cold.

(Dhwani, Dheera and the Old Woman exit.)

POLICEMAN

What now?

POLICEWOMAN

Sandwiches and coffee… *(They move to serve themselves.)*
Mayonnaise has egg? *(Opens a sandwich and sniffs it.)* No,
smells eggless… Thursdays I don't eat non-veg.

POLICEMAN

Eggs you can smell… but, how can it smell eggless?

POLICEWOMAN

Means I can't smell the egg.

---

18 Prayer songs.

(Starts eating. Silence.)

POLICEMAN

Tragic…

POLICEWOMAN

The family wants to move on… The tragic episode of the daughter is a closed chapter now… almost a double tragedy… with the husband trying to immolate himself.

POLICEMAN

She must have been brutally traumatised to see him burning in front of her.

POLICEWOMAN

You think?

POLICEMAN

What are you hesitating about?

POLICEWOMAN

She is feigning, right? The mental thing… she is frightened…

POLICEMAN

Not for herself… She has brass balls. It's that man who tried to kill himself…

POLICEWOMAN

Everyone wants to lead a normal life… Why have enmity with powerful men? … Not needed at all… Those men who were arrested, even if they go to prison now, how long before they come out? And then, it will be blood… I too have children… And I too will be worried if someone will harm them… I am surprised this agreement took this long… always best to avoid problems.

POLICEMAN

Compensation will help.

POLICEWOMAN

Tell you a secret…? Only partial… Rest will be eaten up… It has to pass many tiers before it reaches their bank account. Talked to the man? What is he going to do?

POLICEMAN

Get out of the burns ward fast… He is lying there with bandages… Wants his appointment order at the earliest… wants the local school to be named after his daughter, her statue in it… Has a car to travel in now… armed police to be around them for a few months… by instructions from the boss.

POLICEWOMAN

God's will, she said…

POLICEMAN

Anything else here?

POLICEWOMAN

No, nothing… You take the snacks home… Why waste them… I have the day to myself… What about you?

POLICEMAN

No, I have work… you take them… enjoy with the kids… watch some movie on Netflix. That series is good… *Mai.*

POLICEWOMAN

I have Netflix only on my phone. On the laptop, it is too expensive… What work?

POLICEMAN

I am off to the police station… Last evening, a few men got into an auto and went to settle some enmity in their locality. They asked the auto to stop at a point… got down and started hacking a person who runs a tea stall there… They were armed with sickles… that person managed to run away with minor cuts to his arm, and filed an FIR. We got the auto driver and two of the men…

POLICEWOMAN

Open and shut. Why are you needed?

POLICEMAN

The auto driver is twenty-one years old, a college student, and says he knew nothing about the planned attack. He was flagged down as always to take passengers… They asked him to wait and that's when this happened… says he is innocent.

POLICEWOMAN

Maybe he is…

POLICEMAN

His mother has been transferring money via *Gpay*[19] to the remand home to keep him safe and get him food… 2000 rupees per week… 1000 rupees for the police guard and rest for the boy…

POLICEWOMAN

I pity the mother. It's always the mothers.

POLICEMAN

She has been sitting at the station… She bawled when she saw him in handcuffs… They want me to talk to her…

POLICEWOMAN

About what?

---

19 App for Money transfer.

POLICEMAN

About removing his name from the *FIR*[20] if she can pay two lakhs…

POLICEWOMAN

Two lakhs… She has two lakhs? And you will be doing it?

POLICEMAN

Of course… that's my fucking job, right? Can I say no to my superior? Apparently she is from my community. The woman is a domestic help in one of those apartment buildings. Her employers came to the station too. But what the fuck! Unless she pays two lakhs, he will go to court, be identified, charged with being an accessory to murder and go to jail… fuck his college… fuck his education… fuck his future. Add one to the list.

POLICEWOMAN

What list?

POLICEMAN

Criminals…

---

20 First Information Report (FIR) is a written document prepared by the police when they receive information about the commission of a cognizable offence.

POLICEWOMAN

Fuck! What's tomorrow like for you? Railway duty? Or the police station?

POLICEMAN

Maybe I will see that girl again… This time, I will make her empty her handbag.

POLICEWOMAN

And then… close yourself in the bathroom and smoke up?

POLICEMAN

Must be some excitement… never tried it…

(Silence.)

POLICEWOMAN

I have been assigned to the Minister's security detail.

POLICEMAN

That's lovely… Did you ask for it?

POLICEWOMAN

I am not too excited… let's see.

POLICEMAN

He asked for you, I am guessing… it's a promotion then.

POLICEWOMAN

Let's see…

POLICEMAN

You take care… Pack the snacks… don't forget… *(Moves to exit.)* And congratulations!

POLICEWOMAN

You be safe… *(Policeman exits. She looks at the platter.)* Fuck… *(Starts packing the snacks.)*

THE END

PHOTO: M SIVANESAN

PHOTO: M SIVANESAN

PHOTO: M SIVANESAN

Photo: M Sivanesan

About the Playwright

V Balakrishnan, an alumnus of Shri Ram Centre for Performing Arts (New Delhi) and the National School of Drama (New Delhi), is the founder and artistic director of Theatre Nisha. He has directed over 210 plays, acted in over 160 plays and written more than 15 scripts.

He was awarded the Charles Wallace Scholarship to attend an International Residency with the Royal Court Theatre, London. In 2017, he was awarded the Fulbright Distinguished Award in Teaching (FDAT). In 2018, the Rotary Club of Madras East conferred the Dronacharya Award on him for his contributions to theatre education. In 2019, he won the Hindu Playwright Award for his script *Sordid* and was chosen as a Fellow for the Arts for Good Fellowship 2019 organised by the Singapore International

Foundation. He won the Sultan Padamsee Award for Playwriting 2022 for *God's Will*.

Zero Degree Publishing published four of his plays—*The Curse of Urvashi*, *The Peacock Prince*, *Krishna's Dark Son* and *Dvijottama*—in 2022, and two of his plays—*Amrapali* and *Gallantly Fought the Queen*—in 2023. Most recently, Dhauli Books has published three of his plays — *Sordid*, *Margazhi* and *Arundhati*—as a collection.

www.ingramcontent.com/pod-product-compliance
Lightning Source LLC
LaVergne TN
LVHW091619170726
843492LV00007B/2506